MW00929657

The Cancer That Wouldn't Go Away

A story for kids about metastatic cancer

Hadassa Field

Illustrations by Christina G. Smith

**Including "How to Use This Book"
by child psychologist Rinat R. Green, Psy.D.**

This is a work of fiction. All the characters
and events portrayed in this story are either
fictitious or are used fictitiously.

The Cancer That Wouldn't Go Away
Copyright © 2013 by Hadassa Field
Illustrations Copyright © 2013 by Christina G. Smith

Book Design by Elizabeth Green Musselman
Edited by Sara Mosak Saiger
Art Direction by Sara Mosak Saiger

All rights reserved, including the right to reproduce
this book, or portions thereof, in any form.

ISBN 978-1-300-30317-6
First Edition March 2013
Printed in the United States of America

For Tehilla and Akiva —
you inspired this book.

In memory of Ahuva Rachel Prager —
missed more than words can say.

The Cancer That Wouldn't Go Away

Max's mom had cancer again, and this time, it was not going to go away.

Max's friends said, "Cancer, again? Didn't your mom have that already?"

Max's teacher sent flowers.

Max's grandma called every day.

Max's dad stayed home from work.

Max thought Mom looked fine.

Her hair was nice and long, not like last time, when it all fell out. Mom had looked kind of funny without hair, but Max had gotten used to it.

Now, Mom looked like everyone else. She was not bald, so how sick could she be?

Mom did not even look tired. Last time Mom was sick, she was so tired that she stayed on the couch all day. Now, Mom drove carpool, went shopping and made dinner.

Maybe this cancer thing was a mistake.

Max decided to ask
Mom about it.

"Mom, you feel fine,
don't you?" he asked.

"Pretty good,"
answered Mom.

"Great. I'm glad you are not sick
again," said Max cheerfully.

Mom sighed.
"Honey, I am sick.
The cancer that I had before is back.
Even though we can't see it, it is inside of me. My
doctors found it during one of my exams."

Max could only think of one thing.

"Does this mean I definitely won't get a baby brother?"

Mom shook her head. She looked kind of sad.

"No, Max," she said. "My body is going to be too busy with cancer to do that. Not everyone gets to have a baby. It looks like our family will be just you, me and Dad."

Max was really disappointed.

It seemed like everyone else in the second grade had a new baby, or a mom with a big belly.

All that Max had was a goldfish. A goldfish … and a mom with cancer.

Max spent the next few days telling everyone that his mom was fine.

"She may have cancer, but she can still do everything your mom can do," he told the boy who sat next to him at lunch.

"Lots of famous people have cancer," he told the girl who shared his bus seat.

Everyone nodded.

Max nodded, too, but he didn't feel so sure.

One night, Max burst out crying when dinner was not his favorite.

"What is this all about?" asked Dad,
as Max pushed the chicken around on
his plate using big, angry movements.

"I hate chicken!
I want a baby
brother! I want
Mom to be like
everyone else! I am
tired of cancer!"
shouted Max.

Mom and Dad were quiet. Max was worried.

Maybe he had made Mom feel bad. After all, it wasn't really her fault.

He was afraid to look at Mom and Dad.

When he finally looked up, Mom looked sad, but not angry.

Mom sat down next to Max.

She said, "I am tired of cancer, too. I really wish it were gone, but it is not going to go away. The cancer is in too many places.

"My doctors have lots of medicines to try. My cancer is pretty stubborn, but they think that they can try to beat it down each time it acts up.

"We are all going to need a lot of patience."

Max tried to be patient, but it was hard.

Max was the opposite of patient. He was completely impatient!

Every day, he asked Mom if the medicine was working.

"I hope so, but I don't really know," Mom would answer.

"I don't like not knowing," Max would sigh.

"I know," Mom would say. "But let's try to take things one day at a time. We can try to have a good day today, and not worry so much about my cancer."

Sometimes, Mom looked great. She had energy and she sang along with the radio as she made dinner.

Other days, Mom was tired and she said that everything hurt her.

Max was worried the first time Mom felt that sick.

Mom told him it was okay to feel worried.

She said, "I am having a bad cancer day. I may feel better tomorrow. Let's take things —"

"one day at a time," finished Max. Mom smiled.

Max began to get used to cancer again.

Sometimes Mom felt good.
Sometimes Mom felt bad.
Some days, she played.
Some days, she rested.

Every once in a while, Max would come home and Grandma would be there.

"Where's Mom?" Max would ask.

"At the hospital, getting her medicine," Grandma would answer.

"Right, I forgot," Max would remind himself.

Once in a while, Mom would cry a little bit.

Max didn't like that,
but he could imagine why.

He knew that Mom did not like feeling sick,
or losing her hair again.

One day, he found a
big bag of folded
baby clothes near the
front door. Mom said she
would not be needing them.

She looked very sad that day, and Max
could tell that she had been crying.

Max felt sad, too. He had always
imagined being a big brother.

That afternoon, Max asked Dad
to go bike riding with him,
but Dad said he was kind of tired.

Max looked closely at his face,
and thought to himself,
"Dad looks sad today, too."

No matter what kind of day Mom was having,
she always talked to Max and read him stories.

One day, Mom said, "You know, Max, I've
noticed something! You haven't asked me if my
medicine is working for quite a while now."

"I can be patient, I guess, now that I
am almost eight years old," said Max.

"Remember, one day at a time," said Mom.

"Right," said Max.

Max's eighth birthday was great.
Mom and Dad gave Max a baby kitten!

Max felt very proud and took good care of it.

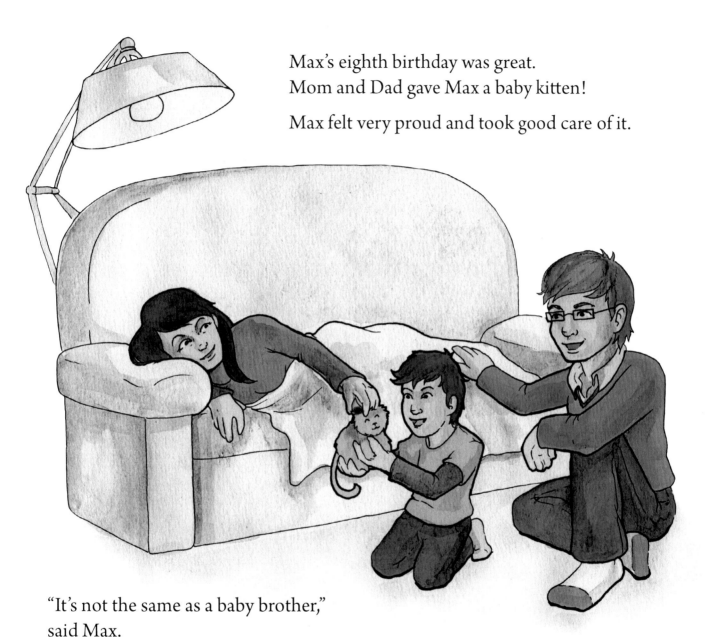

"It's not the same as a baby brother,"
said Max.

"I know," said Mom.

The girl who shared his bus seat said,
"I wish I had a kitten.
All I have is a baby who spits up."

Max smiled.

Max and Mom spent a lot of time together playing with the kitten.

It seemed like she changed and grew a little every day, so every day held a new surprise.

Some surprises were good, like when the kitten played with a ball of yarn for the first time.

Some surprises were not so good, like when the kitten's claws got sharp enough to scratch Mom's favorite chair.

Max brought Mom a soft rag and some polish.

"I guess it's not going to be as easy as we thought," said Max as he gave the kitten some yarn to play with. "Do you think the scratch will come out?" Max asked.

Mom smiled at him. "I hope so,
but I don't really know.
All we can do is try," she said.

"I don't like not knowing,"
Max sighed to himself.

"I know you don't,
honey," said Mom.

"Like I always say,
one day at a time,"
sighed Mom, as she
tried to smooth out
the scratches.

"Yup, just one day
at a time," said Max.

Max laughed, and Mom
did, too.

⇾ *The End* ⇽

How to Use This Book

Rinat R. Green, Psy.D.,
Child, Adolescent and Family Trauma Specialist

One of the greatest challenges a family can face is when a family member is ill with cancer. The situation becomes more complicated when the ill person is a parent of young children. If the cancer then returns in an incurable, metastatic form, the challenge is multiplied.

If you are reading this book, you or someone you know is likely living with this reality.

Most adults have a difficult time coming to grips with the diagnosis of metastatic cancer, let alone explaining it to a young child. The course of events may be unpredictable and confusing. You may find yourself literally at a loss for words. *The Cancer That Wouldn't Go Away*, by Hadassa Field, is a valuable resource for parents, educators, and therapists, which helps facilitate an open and honest discussion with young children about what it is like to live with metastatic cancer.

The Cancer That Wouldn't Go Away is ideal for children ages 4-8, although older children may also find it useful. The book is primarily intended for the stage when cancer has spread, but the prognosis is open-ended. You may find other books more directly useful for early-diagnosis cancer, or for end-stage cancer.

For Parents

Before you introduce this book to your child, it is important that you feel ready for an open and honest discussion about this illness, and for the inevitable questions that may arise. Whether you are the ill parent or the healthy parent, you may be apprehensive. Not every parent is able to handle such a difficult conversation with their own child, and if this is how you feel, your feelings are understandable. It does not in any way reflect on how good a parent you are. It is more important to be honest with yourself and allow the right person to explore this subject with your child, rather than to pressure yourself to do so when you are not ready. It may be more appropriate for you to ask the other parent, an educator, or a therapist to read the book with your child and draw him* into a conversation.

Be aware that this discussion should not be viewed as a one-time, "get it all in" event, but rather as a process which will evolve over time. It is quite common to feel that you didn't answer all of your child's questions properly, or that you forgot something specific that you intended to say. You may occasionally find that the course of the illness has changed and you now need to discuss a new situation with your child. You can always revisit the topic and talk about it further.

Start by taking a few moments to read through the book by yourself, so you can become familiar with the storyline. Scan the story and illustrations for similarities and/or differences to your family's particular situation. These will serve as valuable discussion opportunities.

If there is more than one young child in your family, plan to sit with each child individually at first, so he can freely express

*For the sake of simplicity, the child will be referred to as "him," but of course, the intention is to include children of both genders.

whatever is on his mind, without worrying about what his siblings will think. After each child is comfortable discussing the illness, you can read and discuss the story as a family.

Once these steps have been followed, it's time to introduce *The Cancer That Wouldn't Go Away*.

Find a quiet time of day, when neither of you is too preoccupied. It's preferable to choose a time that is not too close to dinnertime or to bedtime, so that you can have a chance to observe your child's mood after the conversation. Begin simply, by telling your child that you are going to be reading a new book together. Explain that this book will likely cause him to have lots of questions, and that you are looking forward to hearing them. Reassure him that there are no questions that will cause you to be angry, upset or disappointed in him.

As you read the story together, stop at various intervals, especially the ones that resemble the situation your family is going through, and point out the similarities and differences together in a matter-of-fact way. This will help encourage the ongoing discussion.

As your child asks questions or expresses concerns, focus on being open, without overburdening him with unnecessary information. For example, it is perfectly appropriate to tell your child, Mommy is very tired because she is taking medicines that cause her to feel tired. It is not necessary to name all the medicines and the reasons why she is taking each one.

Be sure to accept and validate your child's feelings, no matter how trivial. For example, you might say, I know it's disappointing to see Daddy so tired, especially when you want to play ball with him. But letting Daddy rest is important, because he needs to regain his strength, and sleeping can help him do that. When your child's perceptions and feelings are acknowledged openly, he is less likely to create inaccurate fantasies about what is going on with his ill parent.

One of the hardest tasks of the metastatic stage, for adults and children alike, is coming to terms with the combination of certainty and uncertainty about the future. You'll want to express optimism without conveying unrealistic expectations about the course of the illness. Just as Mom does for Max in the story, the best way you can do this is to acknowledge your child's anxiety about the future, but at the same time, help him learn to focus on the present.

As you read together, allow your child to pause and reflect when necessary. He is listening, but may be working hard to assimilate these new ideas.

While reading through the book, take note of your child's mood. See how he acts over the next few hours, the next morning, and over the next few days. If your child seems agitated or withdrawn at any of these intervals, draw him back into a discussion to help him sort through his feelings. The message you want to convey to your child is that he is not alone, and that talking about the illness is something he can always feel comfortable doing.

This book should not be used in place of therapy, but rather in conjunction with therapy, as befits each individual situation. Ideally, *The Cancer That Wouldn't Go Away* will serve as a springboard for healthy discussion. When your children know they can communicate with you openly and honestly, they will be able to cope with metastatic cancer in the best way possible.

For Therapists

Parents who are dealing with metastatic cancer often find it helpful to consult with a professional, in order to help their child adjust to the diagnosis. If you are a therapist meeting with a young client in this position, you will find *The Cancer That Wouldn't Go Away* to be a useful tool. Take the time to familiarize yourself with the family and medical situation in advance, so that you can lead the discussion comfortably.

If there is more than one young child in the family, introduce the book to them one at a time; this will give each child an opportunity to ask questions and express fears without worrying about what a sibling might think. The goal is to eventually lead the family to be able to discuss the book and situation together. As you progress through the sessions with the family, explain to them that people have different ways of coping with the same situation. One may want to talk about the illness often; another may need to be given more space. It is important to respect these differences and be supportive of one another. Educating the family about coping strategies and general reactions to life's challenges will help them feel more in control of the situation they are facing, and hopefully will enable them to feel more comfortable talking with each other about the illness. It is advisable to leave enough time towards the end of the session for some "down time", so that you can assess each family member's ability to recover from this difficult conversation.

For further explanation of techniques to facilitate an honest, age-appropriate discussion about metastatic cancer, please refer back to the section For Parents.

For Educators

It is not uncommon for families facing metastatic cancer to ask their child's teacher, guidance counselor, or school psychologist to explain the situation to the child's class. If you have been asked to lead such a discussion with a group of children, *The Cancer That Wouldn't Go Away* is an excellent resource to use.

Before you introduce this book to the class, it is very important that you ascertain what the family wants to share. They may just want the class to know that a parent is sick, or there may be more specific information they want the students to be aware of. For example, families may want prospective playdates to know that the medicine the parent is taking for her illness has caused hair loss, and has thereby changed her appearance. It is also critical that you find out exactly what your student knows about the illness, so that you don't find yourself in the uncomfortable position of publicly revealing information that his parents have not yet presented to him. Above all, find out how your student feels about you having this discussion with his class. Make every effort to be sensitive to his thoughts and feelings.

Your primary goal is to help the class understand how metastatic cancer can affect a family, and thereby be more sensitive and helpful to the student coping with the situation. It's important to keep in mind that the subject may evoke strong feelings and concerns in his classmates as well. Make sure to allow time for group questions, as well as individual questions which may arise later, as your students slowly absorb the information. Be prepared for students to approach you days or even weeks later with "one more question." Encourage the class to continue the discussion with you, or with other adults with whom they feel comfortable. Take note of student reactions during the discussion, and over the next few days. Some students may find the conversation upsetting, and may need further counseling.

If necessary, be in touch with their parents to discuss specific concerns.

For further explanation of techniques to facilitate an honest, age-appropriate discussion about metastatic cancer, please refer back to the section For Parents.

In Conclusion

Life with metastatic cancer is undeniably complicated. The course of events is often bewildering for all, and may be especially confusing for children. While the diagnosis is difficult to bear, good communication can help families navigate through it in a healthier fashion. Hadassa Field draws from personal experience to make *The Cancer That Wouldn't Go Away* an invaluable resource for young children trying to make sense of a confusing reality. I highly recommend this book.

—Rinat R. Green, Psy.D.
Beit Shemesh, Israel

Acknowledgments

At age 27, my sister Ahuva Rachel Prager was diagnosed with recurrent metastatic cancer. She wanted to explain the situation to her young children, but could not find any children's books that addressed the issue realistically. This book was conceived in an attempt to help my young niece and nephew understand the confusing diagnosis that changed their world.

A debt of gratitude is owed to many wonderful people, who helped me see this project of love through to completion.

A very special anonymous donor funded most of the cost of publishing this book. Additional funding was provided through close friends, individuals who knew Ahuva, or those who read about the project and were moved to help. Rebecca Winick's bat mitzva project, "Ahuva's Gift," at the initiative of Rebecca and her mother Lesley Winick, accounted for the remainder of the funding. Thank you all!

Our talented illustrator Christina G. Smith brought the story to life in a sensitive and nuanced way. The work she put into this project went far above and beyond, and we cannot thank her enough.

A huge thank you goes to Elizabeth Green Musselman for her masterful layout job. Although the last member to join our team, her cohesive vision for the book made it feel like she was working with us all along.

Emma Alvarez Gibson and Shanna Giora-Gorfajn generously donated their professional editing skills.

Dr. Rinat R. Green lent her professional expertise, as well as her heartfelt encouragement, and wrote a very informative afterword.

My sister Sara Mosak Saiger acted as project manager, art director, and pretty much everything else. This book would not have reached completion without our full collaboration. It was so special for us to work together.

—*Hadassa Field*

Made in United States
North Haven, CT
01 August 2022

22157082R00020